FOR **THE TRIXTER,**
MY OWN LITTLE MONSTER

WALKER BOOKS
AND SUBSIDIARIES
LONDON · BOSTON · SYDNEY · AUCKLAND

This edition published in Great Britain 2007
by Walker Books Ltd, 87 Vauxhall Walk, London SE11 5HJ

10 9 8 7 6 5 4 3 2 1

© 2005 Mo Willems

The right of Mo Willems to be identified as author/illustrator of this work
has been asserted by him in accordance with the Copyright, Designs and
Patents Act 1988

First published in the United States 2005 by Hyperion Books for Children.
British publication rights arranged with Sheldon Fogelman Agency, Inc.

This book has been typeset in Extravaganza

Printed in China

British Library Cataloguing in Publication Data:
a catalogue record for this book is available from the British Library

ISBN 978-1-4063-0807-5 (HB)
ISBN 978-1-4063-1215-7 (PB)

www.walkerbooks.co.uk

YOUR PAL MO WILLEMS PRESENTS

Leonardo

the

TERRIBLE

MONSTER

WALKER BOOKS

LEONARDO

WAS A

TERRIBLE

MONSTER...

HE COULDN'T SCARE ANYONE.

HE DIDN'T HAVE 1,642* TEETH, LIKE TONY.

*NOTE: NOT ALL TEETH SHOWN.

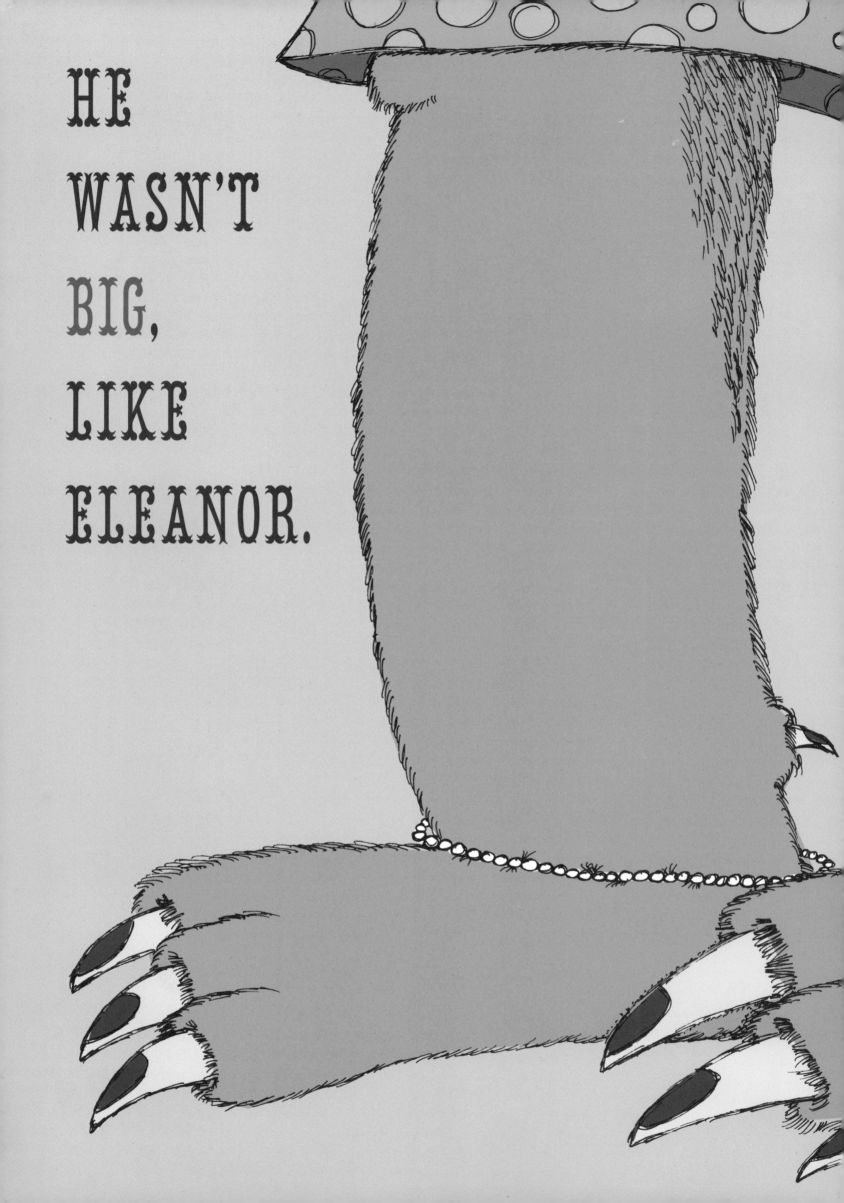

HE
WASN'T
BIG,
LIKE
ELEANOR.

AND HE WASN'T
JUST PLAIN WEIRD,
LIKE HECTOR.

LEONARDO TRIED VERY HARD TO BE SCARY.

BUT...

HE JUST WASN'T.

ONE DAY,
LEONARDO HAD AN IDEA.
HE WOULD FIND THE MOST
SCAREDY-CAT KID IN
THE WHOLE WORLD...

AND SCARE THE
TUNA SALAD
OUT OF HIM!

LEONARDO RESEARCHED

UNTIL HE FOUND THE PERFECT CANDIDATE...

SAM.

LEONARDO SNUCK UP
ON THE POOR,
UNSUSPECTING
BOY.

AND THE
MONSTER GAVE IT
ALL HE HAD.

UNTIL
THE LITTLE BOY
CRIED.

"YES!" CHEERED LEONARDO. "I DID IT! I'VE FINALLY SCARED THE TUNA SALAD OUT OF SOMEONE!"

"NO YOU DIDN'T!" SNAPPED SAM.

"OH, YEAH?"
REPLIED
LEONARDO.
"THEN WHY
ARE YOU
CRYING?"

"MY MEAN BIG BROTHER STOLE OF MY HANDS WHILE I WAS STILL BROKE IT ON PURPOSE, AND IT TRIED TO FIX IT BUT I COULDN'T, TABLE AND I STUBBED MY TOE LAST MONTH WHEN I ACCIDENTALLY I GOT SOAP IN MY EYES TRYING TO THAT MY BROTHER'S COCKATOO DON'T HAVE ANY FRIENDS AND

MY ACTION FIGURE RIGHT OUT PLAYING WITH IT, AND THEN HE WAS MY FAVORITE TOY, AND I AND I GOT SO MAD I KICKED THE ON THE SAME FOOT THAT I HURT SLIPPED IN THE BATHTUB AFTER WASH OUT THE BIRD POO POOPED ON MY HEAD AND I MY TUMMY HURTS!"

THEN
LEONARDO
MADE

A VERY BIG DECISION.

INSTEAD OF BEING
A TERRIBLE MONSTER,
HE WOULD BECOME
A WONDERFUL FRIEND.

(BUT THAT DIDN'T MEAN
THAT HE COULDN'T TRY
TO SCARE HIS FRIEND
EVERY NOW AND THEN!)

THE END

Mo Willems

Described by the *New York Times* as "the biggest new talent to emerge
thus far in the 00s", **Mo Willems** has been awarded two Caldecott Honors
for his bestselling books *Don't Let the Pigeon Drive the Bus* and *Knuffle Bunny*,
and has won six Emmy Awards for his writing on *Sesame Street*.
He is also the creator of Cartoon Network's *Sheep in the Big City*.
Mo lives with his family in Brooklyn, New York.

ISBN 978-1-84428-545-7

ISBN 978-1-4063-0812-9

ISBN 978-1-84428-513-6

ISBN 978-1-4063-0158-8

ISBN 978-1-84428-059-9

Available from all good booksellers